Contents:

I would like to thank James Herbert for setting me on the path of horror writing and illustrating after reading "The Fog".
Without his insight into terror and the supernatural, i might never have experienced what a good scare can do to you.
Also thank you to Mark who is wonderful and puts up with me, my stories and my paintings.
He gives me constant encouragement and help, THANK YOU.

FOR THE LOVE OF HIS SON

Oh how he loved his son. Ever since the day that little bundle was handed to him in the hospital room. He had held him close while weeping for the death of his beloved wife and he had promised there and then that the little boy he held in his arms would want for nothing and would never come to any harm.
Looking down at this little wrinkled face, he placed a solemn oath that until the end of his days they would be inseparable. And he always kept his word.

The years rolled by and the little boy grew with so much love and attention placed upon his tiny shoulders that he doted on his father and wanted to spend every waking moment with him. When he was not in school they would go fishing, play football or just laze around in the garden just chatting about anything and everything. They had so much fun that the little boy preferred to spend time with his father more than he did with anyone else. However as the years rolled by so quickly the young boy found love with others. His father feeling so left out and alone begged him to stay home and be with him always. The young boy was torn. He loved his father very much but he had found a greater love in Annie. He had brought her home to meet his father but his father would just walk into another room and all he could hear was crying. He became embarrassed by what his father was becoming and told him so one night.
His father pleaded, begged but to no avail, his son had told him he was leaving and going to live with Annie. They would survive, they both had good jobs. His father could not take it and as his son turned to leave, in a fit of anger, he

picked up the fire iron stood again the mantelpiece and hit his son with it so hard it killed him with only one blow.
The father watched as his son hit the ground, stood hypnotised while he saw the blood grow and spread out on the carpet. He fell to the ground beside his son, taking his head on to his lap he began to cry and rock back & forth singing a lullaby of old.
Later that night when the last of the tears had been shed, he had fallen into a restless sleep on the living room floor. He dreamt his son was still alive and was waiting for him. His eyes sprang open as a strange noise invaded his ears. He tried to peer into the darkness and when his eyes adjusted, he saw the shadow stood in the doorway. He looked down beside him and realised his son was not there just a pool of congealed blood and the poker he had dropped earlier. He again looked towards the doorway and the shadow was now moving towards him slowly. As the glow from the moon caught the shadow he saw with relief this was his son. He was not dead, but he did look deathly pale or maybe that was just the moonlight shining upon his skin.
He crouched over to push himself up and that was when he felt the sharp crack on the back of his skull. Again and again it reigned down upon his head and as he rolled over onto his back he saw towering above him with the poker in his hand and just before that poker came down one more time he heard.
“Now you can have what you have always wanted father, for us to be together forever. Not in life but in death”

Images of Evil

The smoke in the mirror signalled the return of the darkness. It was a being so dark & heartless that the darkness had been his home for a lifetime of eternity. Once he had walked the earth as a mortal man, but his black deeds had been his doom.
He had hated the darkness and longed for his return to the mortal world and now was the time he had waited for.
The mirror was placed high and proud by its new owner and his time had come to be released and freedom called. It was his time to reek havoc and destruction once again.
The smoke brought him closer to the glass like a guiding hand, to enable him to see what his new world was like and to find his new beginnings. He knew what must be done now.

Jack Reynolds hung the mirror over the fireplace. He liked old and rustic and this item was certainly that. He had been given this by his grandfather who had initially bought this, put it up and did not like the feelings he got from it so had left in his attic for years. The only reason Jack had now got it was because his grandfather had moved into a retirement home. Jack was told by him that if he did not like the mirror he would not be offended if he was to dispose of it.
But Jack had liked it the gold leaf frame which looked old and worn attracted his eyes constantly. The glass was certainly old and mottled which gave it great mystery. Apparently it had been hung in a great hall at one time and when the man disappeared one night his whole estate was sold off. No one saw the man again and many were thankful for that as he was by reputation a mean and brutal man who did not like to socialise with

others apart from when he was drunk. His mouth had got him into many a bad situation but he always seemed to slither out of trouble just as quick. It was rumoured that his money talked and when he waved it in front of someone they took it and matters were laid to rest. The other part of this man's history was noted that when he disappeared and the house items were sold off the house was due to be renovated to accommodate a family.

One of the cellars walls was pulled down and what met their eyes was what had always been suspected about this individual. He was a killer. The body count totalled 30 by the time some of the bone parts had been put in order of man, woman and child alike.

Some were still mummified, proving that they had been recent kills but others were just bones. When this discovery was made the family moved out and the house stood empty and was eventually knocked down totally.

Jack loved looking into the history of items which impressed him, knowledge probably no one else knew about and no one cared about really. But to have things that had history was very special to him. Everything in this house had history and a meaning. His bed was used by Queen Victoria's son he had a chair which was said to have been what Van Gogh had sat on when he had painted his sunflowers piece. He could go on about everything in here but no one was interested. His friends were not interested they had better things to while away their time with, like girls, drinking, sex etc.

The first Jack realised that something was wrong was when he spotted blood on his bed sheets the morning of 20th January 1988. The bed was soaked in it and no matter how he searched he could not find the source of the blood. He had not cut himself at all. He was very shaky thinking that something terrible had happened last night and he could not remember. All he did remember was parts of the dream he had which had disturbed him greatly. He was in a misty shroud of fog, he could just make out that he was stood in some wasteland with trees that were dead surrounding him. The mist felt very creepy and there was a presence he could not see but he could feel and he did not like it.

The next morning he woke with a thumping headache and as soon as he sat upright in bed he promptly threw up. Resting with his arms on his knees he felt very light headed and stayed where he was for a minute breathing slowly in and out.

Clutching the end of the bed he pulled himself up and went to the bathroom.

When he looked in the mirror he could not believe the face that was staring back at him. He staggered back and sat down on the edge of the bath shaking. His face looked ghastly and grey in pallor and it was so thin and drawn, he looked as though he was dying. But that was not the only thing.

His face and his bedclothes were drenched in dry blood. He stripped off and stood in the shower scrubbed him-self until his skin was red raw and wrapped himself protectively in a big bathrobe. He stepped over the bundle of blood-soaked bed clothes and made his way to the kitchen to make some coffee. As he stood waiting for the kettle, he listened to the radio in the back ground. When he heard about the third murder in two days he bent over and switched up the volume. It said three women had been brutally murdered and dumped in alleyways within walking distance of each other and promptly under the nose of the police who were still at the

first murder scene. No one had heard or seen anything and so far they had no clues to who had murdered them. The police were baffled.
The kettle clicking off startled him but he had become very uneasy within himself thinking about what had happened and his state of mind and clothes over recent days. Could he be the one who had done it?
No surely not, he thought. I would know, wouldn't i??
But there was a nagging doubt in his head now along with the pain from the headache. He sat with his coffee at the kitchen table sipping slowly. His mind began to drift away again until he was in the mist that he had dreamt about previously. This time the feeling of an evil presence in the mist was stronger and he became almost hysterical at the thought of whatever it was revealing itself. It was then that he heard it, a small voice from behind him and he stood stock still not wanting to turn and see it.
"One more that is all i need and then you will be free of me and i will walk the earth in freedom once more".
Goose-bump flesh rose on his arms as the raspy voice spoke the words.
What did it all mean? One more, i will be free of it and he will have his freedom again?
The mist began to diminish and he found himself staring once more into his coffee cup. The cold from the mist and the sound of that voice stayed with him haunted him. He walked into the lounge and switched on the television and for a second just store at the screen dazed until the same news broke through about the murders but this time there was pictures. Awful pools of blood in alleyways cordoned off by yellow police tape, DO NOT CROSS.
His mind was reeling he thought he was going to be sick. His heart and head were thudding painfully and the voice played round in his head grating on his nerves. He lifted

his head slightly and the mirror caught his eye and he thought he caught a glimpse of a face. But when he looked full on he could see nothing. That night he stayed awake not wanting to wake up covered in blood from an unknown source again. If he could he wanted to see what happened and not wake up wondering all day what he had done and if he was responsible for these terrible murders. Around 9pm the room had started getting so cold that he could see the breath leaving him as he breathed out. The mirror took on a life of its own and seemed to warp into grotesque shapes and then the mist mingled on the glass starting off very thick and then thinning out as a shape formed from between the mist in front of the glass. He shook his head this was not possible, it must be this damn headache, he thought.
The same voice kept repeating one more, one more. That one more is you.
He clamped his hands over his ears trying to block it all out but it was still so clear, he looked towards the glass and saw the very face of evil staring back at him. But no it was no longer in the mirror it was at the end of his bed. It had escaped the mirror, how? He asked himself.
The figure moved towards him and told him now was the time for him to trade places and find eternal rest and i will walk free amongst the unknowing. They will know me but only when it was too late. The mist surrounded him and the figure and when it began to clear the figure had disappeared but there was something strange and different now. He tried to focus his eyes and all he saw staring back at him was darkness and a small cracked window through which he could see his world, his room, empty, waiting for his return again whenever that may be. He had traded places with the devil and paid the price of

being trapped in a terrible world forever whilst evil reeked its terrible vengeance on the unsuspecting.

Mid Life Crisis or Excuses??

I watch him lay there on the sofa. My thoughts and feelings for him are only of disgust. Once where there was love in my heart for this man, there is now only hate and bitterness towards him and what he has become. The smell of that disgusting aroma he likes to call aftershave, hangs in the air making me feel sick it is so strong.
But does he care......NO.
Why should he anymore they are all the same....MEN. They get what they want out of life, lovely loyal and devoted wife, kids to show that they have the ability to produce and prove they are a man. But then what happens, they start to go a bit strange and change bit by bit.

I know that we women have the inevitable experience of looking forward to the hormonal years. After everything we have had to endure and put up with in life, but do we go strange like this. NO..... this is a definite man thing called MID LIFE CRISIS.

I watched my mum go through the same thing with my dad. I was about 15 years old at the time and I remember it clearly. He had gone to work as my dad and he had come home, well more like a totally different person. For one he had been shopping in his lunch hour he had told my mother, needed to buy some new things. But these new things were for someone more my own age and did not look right on him at all. I remember also that is when all the arguments started. Every night, my mother would plead with him not to go out again and he would just walk past her and slam the door as he went. She would lie sobbing on her bed for hours and he would finally

totter in when the sun was starting to rise.
My dad had always loved cars but I was surprised when he bought himself a sports car and my mother had not been happy because he had spent most of their life savings. The neighbours began to whisper about he was seen hanging around with young girls, taking them for drives in his new car. Making a real show of his self but that was until the day that my mother killed herself. She had gone shopping and from what I had heard there was some gossip mongers who she overheard talking about how her husband had got one of these girls pregnant. The girl had been 18 years old and when she told him he had laughed at her and told her he was not getting saddled with her and a kid, he had a family and was not leaving them for anyone.

The girl had been furious and threatened to go to his wife and expose him. But he had told her that was the last thing she would ever do.
Now when I heard this through a friend of a friend I could not believe that my Dad was such a monster to threaten someone in that way, but they swore it had been true.
Anyway in my mum's case she had stuck it out and my Dad had eventually returned to normal and from what I heard the girl had lost the baby and taken up with some rocker moving to Brighton.

But it is my old man now I look at lounging about on the sofa like he has not a care in the world.
Bastard, how could he? He could he act so normal as though he had not done anything.
How could he treat me like that after all these years of marriage? I had hoped, as in my Dad's case that he would become the same person I loved and married, but he hadn't and I had just about had enough. I was 43 and I had

cooked, cleaned, washed dirty nappies and clothes for the past 20 years and this is what I got in return.
My friend's had told me to glam up and come out with them to the clubs but those days were behind me now.
Even if he thought it alright to cheat on me I could not and would not do the same, even if the opportunity presented itself.
One thing was for sure I would make him pay for the treachery he had bestowed on this family and it would be soon.
I had found out about the affair purely by chance on a shopping trip. I was stood on one side of the isle and the young girl and her friend were on the other side. They had started giggling about her latest conquest and then I heard his name more than once brought up in the conversation, even down to a description of him and his flash car.
I stumbled round to their side and just stood a small distance away so I could get to hear the rest of what was happening.
She totally threw me when she said they had been seeing each other for 3 years and he still would not leave his wife.
I of course got to hear the usual comments I suppose of what a bitch not letting him go, etc and with that I put my basket down and went back to the car. Once inside I sat and cried until my tears dried up and I could cry no more. I was in a total daze and couldn't think straight.
No wonder he was always off on trips with work all of a sudden, getting tarted up to go out with the lads and trying his sudden fumbled attempts at making love. The car he said he had borrowed off a friend who had gone abroad and wanted him to look after it, a likely story.
When I started the car I realised there was only one way to resolve this.

That had been six months ago and I still felt disgust for this man who called himself my husband and I could take no more.

The newspaper headlines for Friday 13th October read:

Local Woman Kills Her Husband in a Vicious Attack with a Knife

She pleaded guilty to murder due to extenuating circumstances and when a medical was done it was found she was going through the menopause. She explained about the affair her husband was having and the shame.
It was later revealed that the car did in fact belong to her husband's friend who had been posing as him to get this girl into bed and when she got pregnant he skipped the country and left the car in his friend's safe hands.
Her husband had spoken to friends about putting some spark back in their marriage and had started to work long hours to be able to take them away on a long second honeymoon holiday and he had started to look and dress a bit smarter so she would still want him.

My Father's Love

All i had ever wanted was my father's love. But he had my brother Leon, his heir and the only thing he ever cared about. Leon and i were twins and when giving birth to us my mother had lost her life. My father had not really cared for her, just as he hadn't for me. All he wanted was a son.

My brother had always been a sickly child where as i grew strong. I was courageous and he was not, we were like chalk and cheese, but my father still loved only one, his son. He hated me because i had the health and strength that his son was denied and for that i was blamed constantly by his increasing silence to me.

I cried myself to sleep most night's just wanting him to hold me in his arms as he did Leon. To praise me as he did Leon, but it never happened.

I fell desperately ill when i was 13 and the doctor did not think that i would make it. My father never came to see me, never asked how i was. He was just worried that i would pass my disease over to his precious son and he would die. So he stayed away.

When i was well i went to see my father and he told me there and then quite bluntly that if i made his son ill then he would send me away forever. I kept in my room from then on, only coming out for food and water. My brother did get ill, but he did not die instead he was sent away to recuperate abroad with rich relatives and i was sent to work in the kitchen cooking and cleaning for him.

I could see my father declining in health when Leon went and he got worse by the day until finally he took to his bed. I called for the doctor because he had banished me from ever coming near him. All he wanted and called for to come was Leon.

After speaking to the doctor i sent word to Leon that father was gravely ill and he needed to return to be by his side.
A week later, Leon returned and went to father's room alone. Leon had changed since being away and not for the better either. When he had walked in the house he had sneered at me with my untidy hair and drab clothes and when i went to hug him, he pushed me away and told me to bring him some wine after he had first visited father.
I heard the argument plainly from the kitchen. My father's voice pleading to his son to come sit by his side, but Leon just laughed and told him he had things to do, more important things than babysitting an old man. I heard my father weeping all night calling for Leon, who never came. In a drunken state had declared he was going out and would not be back until late.
Leon over the next few weeks got in with a bad crowd, constantly drinking and gambling while father fretted and worried about him. But he did not care, he was lost to us. His rich friend's were more enticing to him now but those friend's had bad reputations for causing trouble and this time it was Leon's turn to suffer.
He had brought them all home one night, all drunk they headed towards the dining room where they began an endless round of cards with big stakes.
Leon had winning hands time and again until one of his so called friends accused him of cheating and in a heated argument that spilled out of the room and out onto the driveway turned into a brawl. I grabbed at my dressing gown and ran down the stairs determined to break up the fight.
I stepped between my brother and his attacker just as a glint caught my eye. I did not feel anything at first just like a small jab, but then i felt faint and my heart began to beat

very fast. I looked into the eyes of the attacker and then saw my brother's face swim before i fell to my knees and then to the ground. As i died i heard my father's voice scream into the night my name and how he loved me. He begged me to come back to him but it was too late, at least i had protected his son and heir and i knew right at the end he loved me after all.

One Horror Movie Too Many

John loved his horror movies it took his mind off day to day goings on.
One being the nagging of his wife who was constantly on his case she was always bleating on about something. Belittling him in front of people, humiliation whenever she could and believe it, she could. He always looked forward to when she went to her bridge club then he could put his horror movies on and life was different, fun and exciting.
He sat forward with beer in hand and prayed the vampire hunter to stake Dracula and when he did he almost cheered. John had watched this movie so many times but he loved it and often wished that he could be a vampire hunter and stake the one thing in his life that needed to be staked. But he knew he was tied to her for eternity, a life of sheer hell and damnation. Maybe he could walk out on her, just up and disappear, people did it and the police would be none the wiser. But then she would get all his hard earned money, no this was not the way or divorce, she would fleece him well and truly and he would be left with nothing. But the more he thought about the film and the situation that he was in the more his head filled with ideas until he had settled it right there and then. He would die but live, get away from her but be free to live a life of his own.
If i was declared legally dead but then came back to life again it would be great, but how to do it was the question he kept asking himself. What i need is a vampire, like in the movie, to suck my blood and then i will wake up later and i will be immortal. Maybe i would come back and suck her blood sometime but he did not think he would ever want to

see her again let alone give her the chance of living forever. He put his head in his hands and wished that he could be strong enough to leave. Yes as soon as she walked in the door he would walk straight past her and out. He sat back in his chair with a cigarette in one hand and beer in the other smiling to himself.

He often played these fantasies through in his head and wished, prayed to God whatever he could to have his life back. But no one listened, no one helped, had everyone gone deaf. I have made up my mind this time, he thought, i am going, as soon as she gets home. But there were a couple of hours left yet.

After finishing the cigarette and beer he picked up the local paper and began to read. He flicked the pages without really reading until he got to the lonely hearts page. John liked to read this because it gave him hope there was life out there and maybe also a woman who would love him and take care of him as much as his wife did not.

Some of the ads were funny and as he read them he began to imagine what some of these people may look like and he chuckled. Bet they are nothing like the descriptions they give really, he thought. Then a large ad caught his eye with a large red and black border to make it stand out more. He could hardly believe his eyes, his wish had been answered and he had to get to this address and meet the woman.

John's wife suddenly appeared at the front door as he was getting his coat on and no sooner was she one foot in the door, she started to shriek at him.

"Where are you going?" she asked, "Do you know what time it is?"

"Shut up you shrieking demon," he bellowed back at her, "You will no longer tell me what to do, where to go or whom to speak to. I am leaving and i am not coming back".

He could still hear her shrieking at him as he slammed the door shut behind him. Good riddance, he thought.
John hurried through the streets which were by this time dark and very cold. The wind blew his coat wildly but it would not stop him from getting to his ultimate goal and before he knew it he had found the address he sort and stood looking up at the windows which had a gentle glow radiating from it.
He pressed the buzzer and announced his arrival to the woman's voice on the other end. It was like she was expecting him she did not question who he was or what he wanted. He entered the building to find the woman who was going to change his life forever and that was a promise.
The next day there was a knock at the door of John's home. It was the police to give his wife the grim news that John had been found down by the riverside, dead. There had been no sign of suspicious circumstances and it was thought he had dies of a heart attack. Even though they had not really got on she did love him and she would make sure that he was looked after in death anyway.
John opened his eyes and saw the silk lining of the coffin and nearly shouted for joy. It had worked, he had come back. When he had seen the ad he thought he would get to the apartment and the woman would have been a fake, but she had indeed been a vampire and she had sucked his blood, he had died and now he was back. His plan had worked and he was now in a coffin from which at sunset he would climb out of and start his new life. An immortal life, he sighed as he rested back. It was funny how he knew it was not time to make his escape. Then he realised it was starting to get very warm inside the coffin.

The inside started to smoke and he realised that the coffin was on fire. He screamed as loud as he could but the ferocity of the flames was louder.

“I know we were not close,” she said the priest, “But i am going to make one last final decision for him. He was always watching those nasty horror films and i know he was worried about being buried under the ground and coming back so i thought i would have him cremated and at least that way his soul can rest in peace without any more turmoil.”

Questions & Answers (From The Mind of a Killer)

I am going to tell you what is on my mind, make it plain and clear so you can't say you did not see it coming. I do not want to hide my feelings on what is on my mind. It is nothing personal just a need in me that needs to be fulfilled. Do you mind if I ask you a few questions because to be honest without the answers I do not know why I do this and I need to understand and then maybe one day I can stop killing.
Why do I want to kill you?
Have you done something to upset me or others around you that I hear about?
Have you been bad towards me in some way? Tell me and then I will know.
All I know is that I am not a reasonable person therefore you will know that I just want to kill you, no particular reason, but you will never know why I have chosen you.
When do I want to kill?
All the time, it's like a craving. It's like a smoker who can't have nicotine and once they have had it they feel better. Once I have killed the craving goes away.....for a while anyway.
If you ask when I am going to kill you then that is totally different as I have not quite decided, I can't be pushed into these things. It is a spur of the moment and it happens when it happens.
At least that way I could plead insanity with the courts if I am caught.
I may do it when you least expect it or you may know when I am coming, we shall see.
How do I plan to kill you?
Now that would be telling wouldn't it? But I will just say imagine the most horrible of deaths is what I will bring to you. No mercy whatsoever will be given. I am not that

type of person and you have my solemn oath on that.
You try to think of some imaginable death burning, being eaten alive, feeling yourself drowning. That is mere child's play to what I have planned for you....believe me.
What I have in mind is so chillingly awful, so unimaginable that I dare not even think of it in detail because it scares me. Yes, me. Sometimes when I do think of it I think, "Am I sick enough to carry it through to the end?" And I answer back, "Of course I am".
My childhood was not a good one and I never had anyone close in my life. I used to lock myself in my room and think of ways of torturing and killing and that made me feel good and gave me a purpose in life. Good old days.....
I dream about those times often and I enjoy those dreams, relish in the old feelings and compare them to the feelings I have now. I wake up feeling so good, fit to face the world every day. Now I am older I have made my dreams come true and killing has become my way of life, it still excites me.
What will become of the husk of your body when I kill you? I can sense that you are starting to believe how serious I am, how I mean what I say. I don't know what will happen to your body, what it will look like when I have finished. Maybe it will be eaten away by maggots or some insect with a ferocious appetite, more so than me I suspect. Just blend away into the dust from what you were made.
Do you not think that was a dignified answer to put your mind at rest?
When I strike it will be with the full power of a devil within me a power so make your body suffer will be unimaginable. Maybe I will pour acid into your eyes first so you can't see what's coming, and then you could

say I spared you seeing what was going to happen.

I am now waiting for you, just as you are waiting for me and I believe we now understand each other totally.

You will live forever in fear of me for maybe one second, one hour, one year. I could pounce on you from a dark alleyway, an innocent looking doorway and just take you there and then.

There will be nowhere that you will be safe not even in the quiet of your bedroom, all tucked up safely in bed. Not in the soothing waters of your bathroom pleasures. Certainly not when you are at work where people buzz round you all day, you will never know if I am one of them watching you.

Not in the sanctuary of a church, hoping that God will help you, forgive your sins and cleanse your miserable soul. Because no matter what you do in your miserable little life, day after day, I am there behind you always, watching and waiting, my mouth watering at the thought of your death.

So look for me constantly over your shoulder. You do not know who I am, when I will strike but know one thing.......

I AM GOING TO KILL YOU!!!!!!!!

Regrets Are For The Weak

Are regrets in life for the weak? You can only wonder when you are in a situation that you have time to ponder and think. I have that time now as i lay here, waiting to be operated on, that thoughts have swirled in and out of my mind and i wonder if things could have been done differently, would i have still gone down the chosen path of my now miserable and lonely existence or would my life have gone on a totally different trail.

My wife, what a lovely, warm and caring person she was. Why have i only realised that now? She put up with so much and she stayed with me, until the children left home anyway. Then the only reason i think she went away was the fact of her dying on me. I was told by my own children that i had driven their mother to her death with all the insults and put downs and occasional back-hander's, but she had to know who was boss in the household, right?

My children have not spoken to me now for 10 years and since retiring i hardly see anyone anymore. I suppose they all felt the same that i drove them away with my views and constant opinions of life. Well who cares?

I never used to but maybe i should have done.

I missed Mary so badly when she died. It was like my heart had been ripped out and i could not put it back again. No one knew, i put a shield round me, but i did and i am ashamed to say that i did treat her badly and i should never have done so and for that i regret making her life hell for all the time she was alive. She deserved better.

Could i have shown more love to my children? Of course i could. I could have been there for them, see them grow up, share in Mary's delight at their

first words, their first step, first day at school.
All that is way past due but there is no going back. They hate me anyway so why should i waste my regrets on them. Things come into your brain at certain times throughout your life that do make you wish that you could go back and change things, make things better, different, but not this. It is much too late.
Could i have made more of an effort with friends and work collegues. At the time you do not feel that it can benefit in any way to enhancing your life and prospects, so i pushed them all away. At the time i did not let it bother me but now, yes. It was when they all talked about get together evenings at the pub, family days out all the men's wives that wanted to be friends with Mary and the kids, but i stopped all that and kept them to myself. But i can see now that it was hurtful and they did not deserve to be isolated.
My dear, beloved Mary drive to her death by me and all i can do is repent and hold onto regrets that are much too late to reverse and make better.

Soon my beloved wife i will be in the ground with you and if there is an afterlife we will live a better life, one you do deserve to live, if you will have me.

The operation has finished now and the mortician pushes me back into the cold until the day i can be alongside Mary, buried deep underground but in a higher place (hopefully) together. And i will make good on my promises.
No regrets are not for the weak, they are for people to realise their mistakes and make good on them, even if it may be too late.

So Blue & So Cold

When my father came to us with the awful news of our grandmother's death, I thought my heart would tear apart and never mend. I tried to be strong as I looked in my father's eyes, but I was fighting a losing battle. My father & I had always been close and that closeness extended to my grandmother, his mother.
When my own mother had died giving birth to me, she had brought me up as a mother figure alongside my father. There was also my sister, whom I had never got on with and any spare moment where we were alone she would punch, kick & twist my skin & hair until I howled in pain. I would never turn her in though for fear of more of the same when we shared our room at night. One night she bound my wrists, gagged me and punched me in the stomach until I wet the bed and then she went and told on me the next day and how she had been soaked through because of it. My grandmother had her sussed out, she knew how cruel she was and I had heard her telling my sister a few times that if she ever saw what exactly she did to me she would not sit down for a week. I know my grandmother meant well, but she did not know that every time she had that talk my sister would hurt me more. The first thing my sister asked my father about his mother's death was "Has she left us anything in her will?"
My father looked bewildered and hurt and rushed off to his room and that night I heard him crying, heartbroken and I worried for him more than I worried for myself being left alone with my sister.
The next morning, my father spoke to me and my sister about the last wishes of his mother. My sister was handed a package which she ripped

apart eagerly to find a pair of silver earrings, a brooch and a silver watch that looked very old and delicate. She threw the things down on the table and ripped open the envelope that had her name written on it and scanned the writing within.
Her face paled, she looked at me occasionally with a seething, silent hatred and then packed everything away into the carrier bag they had come from. When she was sat there silent with nothing to say to either of us my father handed me my package with a handwritten envelope stuck to the outside of it.
I could smell the rose water that my grandmother always wore, rising to meet my nostrils and I knew that she would always be here with me no matter what. I opened the letter first which contained 2 pieces of pink paper which she always used. I sat and read what she had written to me.
My Dearest Charlotte
I am so sorry I have had to go and leave you like this, but you know that I will always be with you and one day we will be together again.
Your sister has probably read her letter before you and is under no illusion that I know she hurt you in some way but could not punish her as I did not ever see her doing it and you never told us of the fact, but I saw the way she looked at you and how frightened you were of her. I have told her that I have written a similar letter to her father and made it quite plain that he keeps a close eye on you and takes note of anything she may have done to upset you and punish her accordingly.
I will miss you my dear child and I have left you something that I know you used to love as a child and I had always had you in mind for this item upon my death. Before you open it, I know that you will not have opened it yet I need to tell you that this item has special powers and strange things have happened to people who have owned this

piece. I will not have time to tell you all of the history behind it but you know that when I tell you something I mean it. Owners of this piece have had misfortune in their lives and they believe that this piece has been the cause of it. I have kept this locked away, except to show you, because of that fact.
It was my mother's and her mother before her and so on through the generations. People have made wishes while in possession of this item and bad things have happened. I have not given this to you because I want to harm you my sweet girl, I have given this to protect you. If this is indeed a wish come true piece then you have a wish but must use it wisely to protect your-self from evil of any kind.
Now you may open your gift, guard it well and make the wish count in your favour and may god protect you.
Your loving Grandmother X

I wasn't sure what the letter meant but she believed that what her Grandmother had given her was special and she would heed her words. She looked up at her sister while she closed the letter and gave the letter to her father for safe keeping. Her sister's face was red with anger as I knew she would try to read it herself later. Father placed it carefully in his pocket and pushed the parcel towards her. Inside the pretty pink paper was a medium size blue colour box. I parted the two pieces and inside was grandma's blue and white diamond necklace. I gasped as it sparkled when met by the light, it seemed so alive but at the same time the stones looked so cold and hard. I took the necklace out of the box and held it delicately in my hands and it was like I could feel a small charge of electric making my fingers tingle. I could hear in the background my sister complaining to my father how she should have had that necklace instead of the stupid things she had been left. I was mesmerised by the twinkling stones and totally lost within them. My father's fist slamming on the table brought me out of the hypnosis of the stones.

He yelled at my sister about how ungrateful she was and how he had read his letter from his mother and now understood why Charlotte always seemed to be clumsy and hurt herself & wet the bed constantly. He told her in no uncertain terms that he had never once struck either of his children but if he caught her doing anything to Charlotte then she would be punished severely for it. My sister got up from the table, knocking over the chair and stomped off to the bedroom. By the time the door had slammed, I had put the necklace back into its box and given the box to my father to keep hold off for me. We hugged and cried softly for the passing of our friend.

My sister left me alone for the next few weeks. My father had given me my grandmother's room and that helped a lot. I could lock her out and the noise of her hammering on the door to be let in would have alerted my father.

I had begun to worry about my father, he had become very down and withdrawn since grandmother's death and I was sure he was drinking to. He locked himself away in his room, not going to work and I feared he had been fired by this time. When he was not in his room he stayed out until late and I always stayed awake just to make sure that he was safe and back with us.

Everyday I looked at the necklace lay in its velvet box although I had never taken it out of the box since the day I had been given it. I had read my grandmother's letter many times since that day and still did not really make any sense of it but just knew there was some sort of warning in there.

Life carried on relatively smoothly until my sister's birthday. My father had been out all day and this did not go down well with her, she wanted her presents. She stomped around the house for an hour or so and then began hammering and kicking my door until finally the door gave way. She charged over to me her face so red and angry looking, grabbed me by the hair and pulled me to the floor. I had no time to react and when I tried to struggle to get away it tore chunks of hair from my scalp, so I lay still and let he pull me. She bumped me down the first three cellar steps, and then with her foot she pushed me the rest of the way until I hit the floor. I had banged my head a few times and my head was swimming. As I lay there she ran up the stairs, slammed the door shut and I heard her lock it from the outside. I pulled myself up to the door and hammered wildly and hysterically calling for her to let me out but all she did was laugh. I sat in the darkness hoping that my father would come home and see what she had done and punish her, that I was stronger and could give her a taste of her own medicine. It was futile to hammer on the door, she would not let me out she would just laugh and call me names.

I don't know how long I sat there in the dark, feeling things crawl over my skin and through my hair and not being able to see what they were was a bonus. Then I heard her voice taunting me, telling me that she had the perfect present for her birthday and it should have been hers all along. I suddenly realised what she meant......my necklace. I banged on the door telling her to take it off. It was not hers to wear and she would regret tampering with it. She began to kick the door and laugh and then all went quiet. I must have fallen asleep because the next thing I remember was the sound of the key turning in the lock and brilliant sunshine flooding through the door with more than welcome warmth to it. I blinked my eyes for a few times and tried to focus but it was hard the light was blinding. I heard my father's voice asking me what had happened last night and why was she locked in the cellar. I tried to tell him but it just came out as a hysterical babbling. I could now see what my father was doing he was on the floor next to my sister who was not moving. I crawled from the cellar doorway over to where they were but he told me to stay where I was and not to come any further. He had his head on my sister's chest and then he was moving fast towards the phone. All I heard him say was AMBULANCE and DEAD. What was he talking about, who was dead?

I moved closer to my sister's body and suddenly saw what he meant. The glinting of the sunshine on the diamonds around her neck, her face grotesquely contorted and purple, the necklace was so tight around her neck that it had embedded itself into her skin. I pulled at the necklace but it would not come away from her neck. I looked down at her body and remembered that last night I had wished she was dead for what she had done to torture me and then the letter my grandmother had given to me had meaning.

"If this is indeed a wish come true piece then you have a wish but must use it wisely to protect your-self from evil of any kind."

I had made that wish unwittingly but it was too late to turn the clock back, the necklace had claimed another life.

The Masked Ball

Jeremy was the sort of boy that blended into a crowd. He was never noticed, did not have any friends, it was just like he did not exist.
But all that changed with an envelope that came through his door one morning to invite him to one of his class mate's masked ball.
Jeremy could hardly believe it, he had never had anyone invite him to anything before and he turned the card over and over in his hands almost to make sure that it really existed.
He read the card again for the fifth time.
"Jeremy
You are invited to my party on Saturday night and the theme is to make yourself unrecognisable with the ugliest of masks. Remember no one must know it is you and there will be a prize at the end of the night for the best.
Steven"
I could go there how I am and would be unrecognisable, Jeremy thought. But he was so happy that he began to roll over in his mind what kind of mask would everyone else wear and make himself stand out above the rest of his class mate's for a change.
On his way home from school that night, he knew where he was going to go once his homework had been done.
Jeremy wolfed down his food, did his homework at lightning speed and then informed his parents he was going to pop in on his grandfather.
It was a fifteen minute walk to his grandfather's but he hardly ever came. The place gave him the creeps. It looked like a ruin from the outside and the garden was overgrown and the trees were all dead. A mist lay silently across the pathway and made swirls as he walked his way through it.
Jeremy had only one reason for coming here tonight and he knew that his grandfather had

the key to his success at the party on Saturday night.
He took the large brass door knocker into his hand and banged loudly with it on the wooden door. The sound echoed for a moment and then the creak of the door hinges signalled the arrival of his grandfather at the door.
"Jeremy," he said surprised, "What can I do for you young man?"
Jeremy made his way inside, noting that cobwebs were getting thicker inside the house each time he came.
"I would like to borrow one of your mask's grand-father," Jeremy replied.
His grandfather seemed very pleased that he could be of help to Jeremy and lead him into the sitting room. Jeremy saw all the masks he knew so well adorning the walls.
"There are many to choose from, help your-self Jeremy. They all have stories to tell and come from all over the world" said his grandfather excitedly.
Jeremy pointed to one away from the others locked in a glass case and told his grandfather he would have the ugly one in the case.
"No you can't have that one," the grandfather said frantically, "It is dangerous, it is a death mask and it is told can only bring the wearer a terrible fate, worse than death itself."
The old man turned away from the wall and called to Jeremy to pick a mask and follow him, he had to have his nap now.
Jeremy showed him a solid gold Inca mask and his grandfather nodded at the selection. Jeremy shook his grandfather's hand and told him that he would bring the mask back on Sunday.
Saturday evening came and the party was in full swing. There were some ugly people around, they had all made the effort and not one person knew who the other was.
Jeremy turned up fashionably late wanting to make an entrance that he knew would

be the entrance of his lifetime. He danced, chatted and even had a drink or two until it was announced that the judging would begin. Jeremy knew he was the ugliest there by far when he had taken the ugly mask from his grandfather's cabinet. He had scoffed at what his grandfather had told him about the mask because he knew this was the one he had to have, the one that would get him noticed forever. They would never again ignore Jeremy.
There could only be one winner and when he was handed the prize money he knew that this was his moment. All he had to do was take the mask off now and they would be astonished because it was him.
Jeremy removed his mask in front of the gasping crowd and as he did so, people began to scream and turn away. Surely it was not that much of a shock thought Jeremy.
"It's a trick," he heard one say. Another replied, "He has got a mask on underneath it".
Jeremy could not understand what people were talking about.
"It's me," he shouted, "Jeremy".
Jeremy pushed passed everyone, he had to go to the bathroom, look in the mirror and see what they all saw. When he did, the face of the mask looked back at him. But how could that be, he had taken the mask off.
His face was grotesque it was like it had melted. His lips were peeled back and his nose looked more like a snout. He staggered back from the mirror in disbelief, opened the bathroom door and ran as fast as he could to get to his grandfather's house. When he got there he was greeted by an ambulance and his mother's car parked outside.
He could not let her see him like this so he found a telephone box and called his grandfather's home, his mother picked it up.

"Can I speak to grandfather please, Mum?" he asked.
His mother then replied that unfortunately he had just died. Jeremy asked her how it had happened and she said he had called her to speak to Jeremy about an item that had gone missing. He was frantic with worry and she had decided to come over to calm him down but when she had got here he had a heart attack and died. Now Jeremy would certainly stand out forever, he could never go home he could never go back to school. What he had always wanted had turned into his greatest nightmare. No matter where he went or what he did he would always stand out.

The Window Cleaner

Every Tuesday he came to this house.
The one on the corner of Westwood Pine Avenue.
Today he wished he had not and the times he had previously spent here would be imprinted on his brain for the rest of his life, literally.
Len had been a window cleaner for a good few years now, took it up when he got made redundant from his job in the commercial sector. At first he needed something to do but did not know what until a friend of his started this round and as it was growing was looking for people to employ. He jumped at the chance. At first he hated the cold, damp weather but over time he became hardened to it. As well as building his customer base he became very good friends with his customers and word of mouth built him a very good reputation and then the promise of taking over the business all together when his friend emigrated with his family to the US.
The business grew and grew but he stayed true to his profession and believed that if window cleaning was good enough for his employees then it was good enough for him to keep doing too and it kept him out of the house. Len hated being stuck in there on his own, he had never met the right woman and guessed at the age of 50 he never would.
That was until he met Estella.
She lived in a corner house that he had cleaned windows for a long time. The house looked quite shabby and dirty looking and gave the appearance of either someone who did not like keeping house or someone who lived on her own and just did not have the time.

For whatever reason the inside looking through the windows, looked as bad as the outside and he never wanted to

be in there too long when she went to get her purse.
But he liked her a lot, she was around his age, stunning looking woman who dressed smartly if not old fashioned and she had a lovely personality. She never appeared to go out at all and had never seen any food or other things delivered so she must go out at some point he had thought. He was drawn to her deeply and started to fall in love with her even though she have never shown any signs but friendliness.
There was something about her that really fascinated Len, he could not put his finger on it but whatever it was it was strong. He wanted to show her how he felt but was not good when it came to chatting to women on a nature other than friendship.
Len had decided this Tuesday as normal he would go and clean the windows and ask her out for a drink.
With a strange nervousness he made his on Tuesday to her house. As he began to climb the ladders he noticed that all the curtains were shut which was very unusual. Len put his bucket on the end of his ladders and as he went to get the sponge out he thought he heard a small whimpering noise. He strained to listen and try to make out where it was coming from, it sounded so far away but so close somehow. Nothing else came so he started to clean the windows, whistling as he normally did. Then it came again and this time it came quite a bit louder. Len was startled and it sounded just like when he had gone rabbit hunting once and the rabbit had been caught in one of the traps. The noise had been awful and the sound he had heard moments ago sounded just like this.
Len edged his way down the ladder and as he did he saw the bottom curtains slide open and Estella's face appear at the window. She beckoned to him and before he knew it the front door was open and she was

standing on the threshold. She had tidied herself up a bit and it looked to him she was trying to impress, someone. As he edged closer to her he caught a faint whiff of perfume and gazed into her eyes. It was then that he saw what he did not want to see.
Pure plain evil blazing in those eyes, the whites were red and looked almost black but there was something else burning in that soul of hers and he was not sure if he quite understood what pure hatred looked like. But here it is right in front, the snarl on her lips. Those luscious red lips. He suddenly realised his mind was wondering and he felt like he was almost being hypnotised and that he did not like. But could he tear himself away from this temptress. Funny that temptress, dressed how she was, but never the less, she was hypnotic and could not help but want to kiss those cruel looking lips and so he did. He was surprised, she did not recoil or pull away at all she was actually savouring the moment just as he was and their fury of passion led them into the house and to the bedroom.
When he was in the bedroom, out of the corner of his eye, he could see that the room was a complete shambles just like the downstairs. But there was something different up here a strange musky smell that he could not place. She pushed him onto the bed and began to strip in front of him. Len wanted her so badly and it looked as though today he was going to get his wish.
When Len woke later, he was covered in sweat and looked cautiously around the room, not wanting to wake his sleeping partner. The corners of the room were very dark and unnervingly so. He felt as though there was something hiding and moving about, watching him, but that was stupid. He had just made love to a woman for the first time ever and what a woman. He gazed at her sleeping next to

him, god she was beautiful. The cruelness in her face that he saw earlier was now gone. What had come over her he did not know and really did not want to know.
Len settled down on his pillow ready to get some more sleep before getting going when he noticed a movement low down on the other side of the room. He sat bolt upright and peered into the darkness. Maybe it was imagination, the flickering of the street light outside but he kept on staring. There it was again but this time there was more a shadow in the doorway, a large shadow one hand on the door frame and one hand in its pocket. He fell into a total panic, he had been suckered in and she was married and he had come home unexpectedly. He shook Estella to wake her. He eyes opened very quickly and she smiled at him with the same evil in her face as before. She raised herself up onto her elbow the covers dropping away from her as she did and it was then he saw the two marks on her neck. He felt the presence of the shadow behind him he could feel the warmth of the thing's breath on his neck.
As the shadow bit into his neck and pulled muscle and tissue away as though tearing he saw that Estella smile, fangs showing, licking her lips for her turn.
Just my luck, he thought, to find the woman of my dreams and she turns out to be a vampire.

The Woman who Loved to Walk in the Rain

When she opened her eyes, greyness was all she knew. It was disorientating: no, more than that still – it was *distressing* – not to know anything about herself other than that she was somewhere grey. Walls of no particular colour other than that of the weak light that filtered through the closed curtains lurked at the periphery of her vision. This was a small room that she found herself in, small and square. She was lying curled on a bed, a sagging mattress and a musty quilt lay beneath her. The pillows beneath her head were old and so thin as to be useless. On the far side of the room was a small toilet & basin. She tried to sit up, and her head swam so violently that it seemed to want to roll free of her neck. The room span and she felt she may be sick, but the feeling faded shortly after she managed to hold herself immobile in a crouching position. She held her fragile head in her hands. In a way this was like being born, she thought crazily, as tears ran slowly from her eyes. She had no memories previous to opening her eyes, she had no name and no identity and no life, and if she did have then she couldn't remember them. She was alone, in a grey room with a sore head. Was this a hotel room? If so, she can't have paid much for it. It looked bleak and dreary and so very small. If she had been standing, and soon she hoped she would be, then stretching out her arms to either side would bring her into contact with opposing walls, and if she turned in a circle she would almost to be able to touch every wall in the room as she did so. There was a doorway beside the head of the bed, and it had a keyhole in it. She would search her clothing for a key when she felt able to, assuming that the door was locked. If not she could just walk straight out… and then what? The idea of walking out of the room when it was all she knew was somehow intensely distressing for her. Anything could be beyond this room...Anything. She raised her head to face the window. Thin, floral curtains were pulled shut against the weak daylight. Thick bars lay beyond the curtains, making the room seem more ominous. Depending on the time of year, it must be late afternoon or evening, for the daylight was definitely in retreat. She stood slowly, unfolding her legs onto the floor like a newborn creature attempting to walk for the first time. She was a grown woman there was no need for her not to know how to do this. She looked down at her own body as she moved, at her long legs, her bare feet, her body hidden beneath a thick black jumper, her long elegant hands, nails bitten short. This is me, she thought, as she raised herself slowly to her full height, a sensation so disorientating that she thought she might never stop rising, that she would float upwards until she touched the ceiling of this grey room and, perhaps, rise through it. But all she wanted to do now was make her way to the window, on legs that felt weak and like fluid, and to take a glimpse at the world that waited beyond the confines of her safe and unknown room. She veered dizzily, almost colliding with the bed, on the short walk, but then she was stood with the curtains in her hands, and she parted them hesitantly, her breath and heartbeat racing. There wasn't much to see. Long rolling flat fields and in the distance were mounds of hills, all dark and colourless. Above the distant fields & hills, the sky was a featureless slate grey. If she had expected anything of the world beyond this room; revelation, or even a gentle reminder of who she was supposed to be, it wasn't to be found. She turned away from the barred window, and as she did so, she noticed in the weak and fading daylight, a small mirror hanging in the shadows beside the wardrobe. She had to step right up close to it to make out anything other than shadowy blurs. That was her face, reflected in the glass mere inches from her eyes. Her dark hair curled over her forehead. Her large, dark eyes searched inquisitively. Her lips parted in breathless amazement as she saw herself for what may as well have been the first time. *So that's me*, she thought as her fingers traced the outline of her reflection, *but who am I?*

She picked up the mirror and turned it in her hands, before throwing it savagely across the room. It hit the wall with a loud thud before dropping to the floor and splintering into tiny pieces. She didn't know why she had done that. She felt angry and confused with herself. Her brain was jumbled and it gave her a headache trying to focus on one particular thing. She slumped on to the bed and sat there as if she was in a trance. Just like the way people would describe a sulky child of looking when they were told off.

Suddenly an image came into her head of two small children. All dressed smartly and waving, as though actually waving at her. Just as quick as the image had come it had disappeared. She felt a strong sense of loss at losing the image as though she should know these children. But try as hard as she might she could not say that she had even seen the children before, let alone knew them.

She curled herself into a ball on the floor and rocked gently back and forth, a smile spread across her face, not the smile of joy or happiness though. A smile filled with pain and sadness.

A simple longing to know who she was where she had come from, and why she was here alone and so unhappy. Getting up from the floor, she made her way to the door and grabbed hold of the handle. Her hand shook badly and she felt very weak. The effort it took just to turn the handle a slightly, seemed to drain her remaining strength. However, determination was on her side and she managed to turn it slightly more until she heard the lock had freed itself. She pulled the door towards her but nothing happened. With a sudden urgency to be free, she rattled the door back and forth but the lock wouldn't give. It would not allow her to be free. She let go of the handle and stood like a statue, with tears streaming down her face. She felt as though her heart was breaking. Folding her arms around her chest, she began to walk backwards and forwards in the tiny room, suddenly feeling as though the room was closing in on her. Now wanting to scream, beg, plead. Anything just to be able to get out in the fresh air, breathe it hard into her lungs. Feel her chest expand and hurt from holding it in for so long and not being able to let go of it until she had absorbed every single drop of it.

Suddenly feeling very tired, she lay down on the bed, turned on her side, curling into a ball and drifted into a fitful sleep.

She tossed and turned, sweat running down her body as she firstly mumbled quietly, mouthing things in her dreams only she could understand. Then the words became loud and coherent.

She was begging to be left alone, sobbing pitifully. Then her eyes were open. Woken suddenly from her dream state, was it by a noise or was it simple by whatever had been in her dream. She could not remember. Pulling the covers up under her chin, she trembled slightly as the perspiration on her body suddenly became cool. It was dark now outside her window. She didn't know what the time was she had no way of knowing. No clocks were in the room, no wristwatch wrapped itself around her arm. But she didn't care any-how she knew that whatever life this had become for her was more like a prison. A living hell and she wished she had the answer to get out of it. She closed her eyes once more and slept soundly.

When she woke in the morning there was a food tray by the side of the bed.

Who had put it there she did not know but she felt suddenly very hungry. While she was eating she was sure that she heard movement outside of the door but it was so faint she could not be sure, she also thought she heard the faint sound of music but again it was so faint it did not seem real at all. Maybe it was just in her head she did seem pretty jumbled most of the time and her head felt continuously cloudy. Just like now as she drank her tea, she felt very light headed and suddenly she dropped the cup she was holding and the tray that was balancing on her lap fell to the floor with a loud crash. As she lay back on the bed she noticed that her tiny mirror had been replaced with another.

It was dark again outside when she woke and her tray had been removed and the floor was still glistening with the water used to clean the floor. The last thing she remembered was dropping her tea and tray and then nothing. Had she been drugged? Who would do such a thing?

She became very frightened at the thought of being trapped in her unfamiliar surroundings and curled up into a ball on her bed and rocked back and forth. It helped calm her, made her think straight as straight as her head would let her think. It constantly felt fuzzy and it swam with any sudden movements. So she sat and she just rocked until finally the dawn of a new day emerged

and she was so exhausted she fell asleep once more.
When she woke again she saw the light was fading and she still felt no better. What was wrong with her? Why did she not remember anything? Not even a glimmer of who she was or where she came from.
She had a blinding headache and there was a slow red mist forming clouding her vision. She pushed herself off the bed and hit the wall where the mirror was and knocked it to the floor, shattering it into small, sharp fragments.
She picked the fragments up and caught a glimpse of herself in the mirror and she knew she could not take anymore of this uncertainty and not knowing.
The report and finding of the coroner was that patient No167 had slashed her wrists and throat so badly that even if they had been able to have saved her at The Lawns Asylum, she would have had no feeling in her arms ever again and she would have been so disfigured that no amount of surgery would have put her back together again. From the profile he had seen from the asylum on this patient she had lost all memories of her former life, she was in a total world of her own and a manic depressive. She had attempted suicide before and that is why she had been admitted to the asylum for her own protection by her mother. It was said that her father's death had triggered the depression that had just spiralled out of control. There was one thing that confirmed her level of sanity at the time she committed suicide was that she had also plucked out her own eyes with the shards of mirror before cutting her wrists and throat.
The orderly that put the mirror in the room for her has been suspended pending an investigation. He said he had done it to try and help her remember who she was if she could see herself.

MADNESS

I scream & shout
And pull my hair out
But it never does any good
And now I only wish I could
Have the courage to put the misery I endure to a close

Just once, that's all it would take
To beat the monster at his own game for sanities sake
To beat him and bury that axe in his head
And carry on hitting him until he is dead.

For the twelve years since we first met
It has always been the fist I would get
Not to speak out of turn, or speak at all
I just wish he was not so big, strong and tall.

I wait until he is sleeping
Then go get the axe and back I am creeping
To stun him slightly to make him immobile
Then to let the years of anger take over for a little while.

I hit and hit and feel like I am never going to stop
My brain feels as though it will explode and my heart pop
It feels so good to have my revenge
For the torture and suffering I have to avenge.

After my work is done
I look at his lifeless body and know he is gone
My life is now my own
But my chance of freedom I have blown.
The police cuff me and take me away
They tell each other that it was probably self defence,
That made me snap with him today
I will hold my head up high and not cry
For I knew the monster had to die.

www.ingramcontent.com/pod-product-compliance
Ingram Content Group UK Ltd.
Pitfield, Milton Keynes, MK11 3LW, UK
UKHW041833200726
13854UKWH00003BA/1111